A Pirate Story

Mythical Creatures

Contents

A Pirate Story 2
Mythical Creatures 25

A Pirate Story

By Debbie Croft

Illustrated by Stephen Axelsen

Characters:

Narrator

Pirate 1

Pirate 2

Pirate 3

Captain Immaculate
captain of the cruise ship, Lotsabucks

Miss Twinkletoes
entertainment director on the cruise ship, Lotsabucks

Narrator

Day in, day out, Pirate 1, Pirate 2 and Pirate 3 squabbled about which of them was going to be the richest pirate in the world. Word was out that there was a hidden treasure on Plunder Island – a treasure that had the potential to change one of their lives forever!

Pirate 1

Arrrrh! 'Twill be I who uncovers the ancient chest, filled ter the brim with gold and silver!

Pirate 2

Well, I've been a-piratin' much longer than ye, so I'm bettin' I will be the lucky one!

Pirate 3

Naah! I'm a-thinkin' yours truly will get it. I've decided there's to be no more buccaneerin' for me.

Narrator

Their old pirate ship was tossed about on the waves for several days, as it headed in the direction of Plunder Island. One morning, as the pirates stumbled out of their bunks, Pirate 1 noticed something was wrong – seriously wrong.

Pirate 1

Look! There's water comin' in through the hull!

Pirate 2

So 'tis! What are we gonna do? We can't swim!

Pirate 3

Shiver me timbers! We could all end up provin' you correct if we don't do somethin' fast!

PLUNDER
ISLAND

Pirate 1

I've got a bucket. I'll keep bailin' the water overboard, like an unwelcome visitor!

Pirate 2

That sounds like too much work ter me! If we soak up the water with this ol' rag, we can just carry on as usual.

Pirate 3

And if we use our brains, we can have that there luxury cruise ship on the horizon, and take ourselves to some exotic port! Who knows, perhaps we can all be extremely rich pirates without even having ter find any treasure.

Narrator

They all looked in the direction of Pirate 3's bony finger. And there it was – the largest and most magnificent cruise ship you could imagine.

The pirate ship limped towards the huge cruise ship, *Lotsabucks*. But by the time it drew up beside the graceful, floating hotel, the pirate ship was sinking. The pirates scurried to the highest point, clinging to the mast and life itself.

Pirate 1

Blimey! There'd be a close call!

Pirate 2

Yer can say that again! But what do we do now?

Pirate 3

Arrr! This is where we sound really threatenin' and yell fiercely! Someone from the big ship might 'ear us.

Narrator

But before the pirates could so much as take a deep breath, a booming voice from a loud speaker on the main deck of *Lotsabucks* bellowed in their direction.

Captain Immaculate

Attention! Attention! Who is your captain? What is the purpose of your journey?

Pirate 1 *(pointing at Pirate 3)*

He is! And we're all comin' aboard your ship!

Pirate 2

Our ship's a-sinkin'!

Pirate 3

From one Cap'n to another, please help us!

Captain Immaculate

Well, pardon me, but you can't just "come aboard" my ship! This is a cruise liner, and all my passengers are very special and elegant people!

Pirate 3 *(yelling)*

We's all pretty special, too, sir! 'Specially smelly at the moment! Yo, ho, ho!

Pirate 1

Aw, come on, Cap'n … where's yer compassion?

Pirate 2

P'rhaps we can do some odd jobs fer a few days 'til we get ter the mainland!

Captain Immaculate

I'm sure that won't be necessary, but …

Narrator

Suddenly, Miss Twinkletoes, the ship's entertainment director, appeared next to the captain.

Miss Twinkletoes *(interrupting)*

Excuse me, Captain Immaculate, but an urgent situation has developed with our act for tonight's on-board entertainment. I have just been advised that the star performer has become ill and won't be able to perform. Can you recommend a replacement act?

Captain Immaculate

Right now, I have my own "urgent situation" to attend to, Miss Twinkletoes. I'll resolve your problem a little later.

Miss Twinkletoes

I'll advise my staff that the problem will be solved in time for tonight's show. Perhaps we can pick up a new act when we get to the next island.

Narrator

Meanwhile, Captain Immaculate arranged for the crew to lower a lifeboat into the water. Without further ado, the pirates clambered into the boat as the last couple of metres of their ship's mast disappeared under the water. They were hauled aboard the cruise ship and dumped unceremoniously onto the deck.

Captain Immaculate

Excuse me, er, gentlemen. My passengers are very wealthy people and have paid good money to be pampered by my staff. They won't appreciate ruffians such as you being on board. For this reason, I must ask you to remain in a secret location on the ship.

Pirate 1

That's okay, Cap'n.

Pirate 2 *(looking around)*

Yeah, we don't mind. We reckon we can tolerate these 'ere conditions for a night or so!

Pirate 3

That'll be fine, Cap'n. You let us know if there's anything we can do in return. We're pretty clever with our hands, yer know!

Narrator

Within a short time, the ship docked at a small tropical island and the passengers disembarked. While they were away, the captain shuffled the pirates into a tiny room on the upper deck.

Captain Immaculate

The door will be locked, and you must remain quiet. I will have the kitchen send you some refreshments. And, er …

(sniffing the air and screwing up his nose)

perhaps tomorrow I should organise a bathroom and some fresh clothing.

Pirate 3 *(winking at the captain)*

Aye, aye, Cap'n. But we don't need no fussin' and botherin' – we're just grateful fer yer 'elp!

Narrator

Before long, the passengers returned from their tropical island excursion. They swanned along the passageways with their designer bags containing expensive souvenirs. In no time, the ship had set sail again, and people went about enjoying the afternoon activities offered as part of the luxurious lifestyle on board *Lotsabucks*.

Miss Twinkletoes *(thinking aloud)*

I wonder who the captain has organised as a replacement act for the stage show? I was rather hoping they were already on board. Perhaps they are just looking around this spectacular ship!

Narrator

Miss Twinkletoes unlocked the dressing-room door in readiness for the performers, but reeled back in surprise. Three scruffy faces peered at her from their relaxed positions on the upholstered recliners.

Miss Twinkletoes

Oh, my goodness, I didn't realise our new act for tonight was already here! I've been waiting for you to arrive. But the agency didn't mention that you'd look so unkempt. Never mind, that's just part of your act, I guess!

Pirate 1

But … but … what act?

Pirate 2

Shiver me timbers, what's goin' on?

Pirate 3

Arrrr! Tonight? Tonight did yer say?

Miss Twinkletoes

Yes, that's right. You'll be performing for us tonight! The agency would have explained that to you.

I think our passengers will really enjoy your act. I sense it will be something very different!

And now, I'll leave you, er, gentlemen, to make your preparations for the show. Good luck! I'll see you at eight!

Narrator

Miss Twinkletoes closed the door. She spotted the captain in the passageway.

Miss Twinkletoes

Thank you, Captain. All is in place for this evening – although the entertainment could be very interesting!

Captain Immaculate *(looking suprised)*

Very well – I'm pleased everything is under control.

Narrator

Back in the dressing room, the pirates were busily trying to think of a plan.

Pirate 1

What on earth are we gonna do? We ain't no "act"!

Pirate 2

This luck of ours could go pear-shaped real easy!

Pirate 3

Yeah … we'll have ter come up with somethin' clever … Wait a minute … This place is loaded with posh people! Don't yer see? We stand ter make more money 'ere than if we found the treasure on Plunder Island!

Pirate 1

Yeah, maybe so. But what are we gonna do?

Pirate 2

We can't dance, we can't juggle, and we ain't no acrobats. So what's left?

Pirate 3

Er … um … well then, we'll sing! We'll sing some of them ol' sea shanties what we've been singin' fer years!

Narrator

On the stroke of eight o'clock, the show began.

Pirate 1

Arrrr! Good evenin' ladies an' gentlemen.

Pirate 2

Welcome to the *Lotsabucks* show!

Pirate 3

You all must have lotsa bucks and we're hopin' to make lotsa bucks! Yo, ho, ho!

Narrator

The audience was horrified at the scene before them. They had expected something very cultured, not this dishevelled act.

Some of the ladies in the audience were so disgusted, they stomped towards the door, clicking their stiletto heels as they went; others placed one hand over their pearl necklaces in shock and disbelief.

But then people stopped in their tracks, mouths agape. From the stage drifted the most beautiful harmonies, a melodious arrangement of sea shanties telling heroic tales of life at sea.

There was wild cheering and loud applause for several minutes. Then Captain Immaculate took the microphone.

Captain Immaculate

What a performance! Surely this act deserves our extra appreciation. Let's pass the bucket around. Come on, dig deep and be generous!

Narrator

Within minutes, donations had flooded in for these somewhat unsavoury characters.

When the encore was over, the captain made an announcement.

Captain Immaculate *(importantly)*

Pirate 1, Pirate 2 and Pirate 3, I ask you to accept lotsa bucks, from *Lotsabucks*! And now, I would be honoured if you would join me at my table for supper. But perhaps you would like some time to freshen up first?

Mythical Creatures

By Debbie Croft

Illustrated by Gregory Baldwin

Characters:

Radio Talk-back Host

Student 1

Student 2

Student 3

Student 4

Student 5

Radio Talk-back Host

And it's a very good afternoon to all my listeners. Thanks for tuning in to our discussion topic for today – mythical creatures. Some of you may like to call in and tell us about an awesome vision you have experienced, while others will want to explain why they believe these creatures simply do not exist, except in our imaginations.

First on the line this afternoon is a group of students from Westbrook Primary School. Hello, girls and boys. I believe you have recently had an experience with a mythical creature! What would you like to share with our listeners?

Student 1

A group of us were camping,
To the river flats we went,
Where we saw the strangest image
As we looked outside our tent.

Radio Talk-back Host

What did you see? Sounds rather fascinating to me!
Please give our listeners a little more detail.

Student 2

We saw this monstrous creature,
Come galumphing through the trees,
As the darkness fell, it tired,
And dropped to rest upon its knees.

Student 2

It made the weirdest noises,
Somewhat like my father snoring,
It went on and on 'til midnight,
By which time 'twas rather boring.

Radio Talk-back Host

Oh, my goodness! This is really interesting. I wonder what our other listeners are thinking? What else can you tell us about this creature?

Student 3

I peered into the darkness,
Not quite sure what I would see,
And quickly found two big bright eyes
Were staring back at me!

Student 4

Yes! One was blue and one was green,
They shone like giant stars,
And twinkled in the dark night sky
Out in space somewhere near Mars.

Radio Talk-back Host

Are you really sure you didn't just imagine it? That's happened plenty of times before you know! Tell us some more about what this "thing" looked like.

Student 5

It had a really shaggy coat,
With straggly, matted hair,
Its grooming was disgraceful
And it didn't seem to care!

Student 1

Its face was somewhat gentle,
And its lashes were quite curly,
Its nose tipped up, its ears hung down,
Its teeth were sharp and pearly.

Radio Talk-back Host

Well – what did this thing do during the night? Did you get any sleep?

I don't believe many of our listeners would have felt like nodding off with that monster lurking about outside the tent!

Student 2

It seemed that sleep escaped us,
Things didn't feel quite right,
So we huddled close together,
Downright stunned by this rare sight.

Radio Talk-back Host

You must have been petrified! Did this creature move around during the night, or did it just sleep?

Student 3

The creature dozed beneath the trees,
And no one said a word,
We just watched from where we hid
'Til eventually it stirred.

Student 4

It stood up on its stout hind legs
And reached towards the sky,
At full stretch it seemed likely
It was three whole metres high!

Student 1

It stomped along the river bank,
The wildlife quickly scattered,
We didn't venture from the tent,
Our lives were all that mattered!

Student 2

It clambered to the water's edge,
To quench its mighty thirst,
And then it guzzled, gulped and burped,
Until we thought it had to burst!

Radio Talk-back Host

And you really believe this creature exists?
I'm almost sure there are lots of listeners
out there who would doubt that very much!
However, carry on …

Student 3

No sooner had it finished
Than it turned and looked our way,
And quickly hurtled up the bank
To our exclamations of dismay!

Student 4

It made a spiral pathway
As it pranced around our tent,
I didn't take my eyes away,
As round and round it went.

Student 5

And then it struck us that it might
Be wanting food to eat,
And so we tossed some meat outside
In pieces near its feet.

Radio Talk-back Host

My, my … That was a mighty courageous decision – don't you think? What happened next?

Student 1

Well, first it crudely sniffed the ground,
Then with a hasty calculation,
It vacuumed every morsel
In the smoothest operation.

Student 2

I barely could believe my eyes,
I thought it was a joke,
But next I knew it filled its lungs
And belched out puffs of smoke!

Student 3

The creature's nostrils tweaked and twitched,
Its eyes welled up with tears,
It looked at us and seemed to smile,
Which lessened all our fears.

Radio Talk-back Host

How did you feel? Were you jittery? Afraid?
Nervous? Or just plain petrified?

Student 4

Although there was no evidence
That making friends was planned,
We felt a strange connection
With this creature of the land.

Student 5

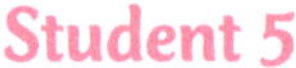

By now the light around us
Had a peaceful, silvery glow,
And swirls of mist came rolling in,
From where we did not know.

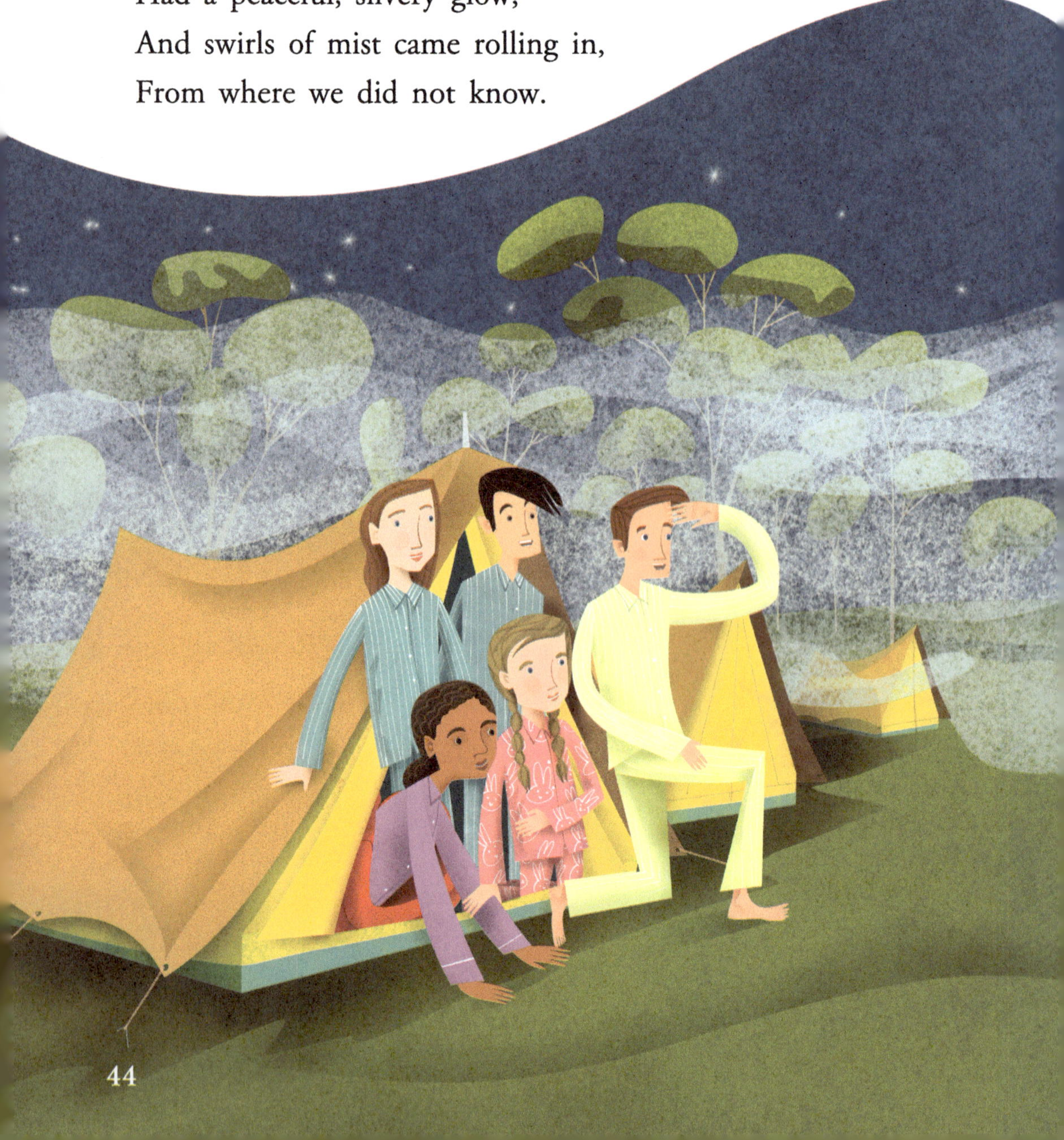

Student 1

The fog enveloped everything,
The landscape was transformed,
But then the rays of sun peeped through
And the grass and trees were warmed.

Student 2

Our eyes all scanned the river bank,
In the quest for one more glance,
But now the beast had disappeared,
We'd had our only chance.

Radio Talk-back Host

So, did this creature really exist? Do you think you will ever see it again?

Student 3

Well, we were left to ponder,
Had we witnessed something rare?
Or was this just a fantasy
And never really there?

Radio Talk-back Host

Well, listeners, you can make your choice!
Is this tale fact or fiction?
Is this creature truly real,
Or based on pure conviction?

I'll be back again next week,
So call me with your thoughts,
But I don't want to hear about
More mythical reports!